Mommy, Do I Have Black Girl Magic?

Written by Ti-Tianna Smith
Illustrated by K&K Publishing

Mommy, Do I Have Black Girl Magic?

Written by Ti-Tianna Smith
Illustrated by K&K Publishing

ISBN-13: 9781686775802

Acknowledgements

I would like to express my special thanks of gratitude to my mother, grandmother, and aunt, Wyconda Green, Gail Wilson, and Sheimeka Webster; and my fathers, Dwayne Green, William Johnson, and Esteven Smith. For instilling in me the faith, strength, courage, and confidence to submit to my purpose. To my husband, Joseph Loyd, and daughters, X'Zarianna Walker and Jah'Zara Loyd, you are my EVERYTHING and my REASON. I love you all!

The purpose of this selection is to promote self-awareness, self-confidence, and self-acknowledgement to females of color. Being a mother of two daughters and a member of a family full of STRONG BLACK FEMALES, I see the need to constantly remind and reassure young females how special they are, AS THEY ARE! This is a colorful selection that mothers, grandmothers, aunts, daughters, nieces, and granddaughters will enjoy together!

Disclaimer: YOU ARE ENOUGH!

Mommy, Do I Have Black Girl Magic?

Written by Ti-Tianna Smith

Illustrated by K&K Publishing

Mommy, Do I have Black Girl Magic?

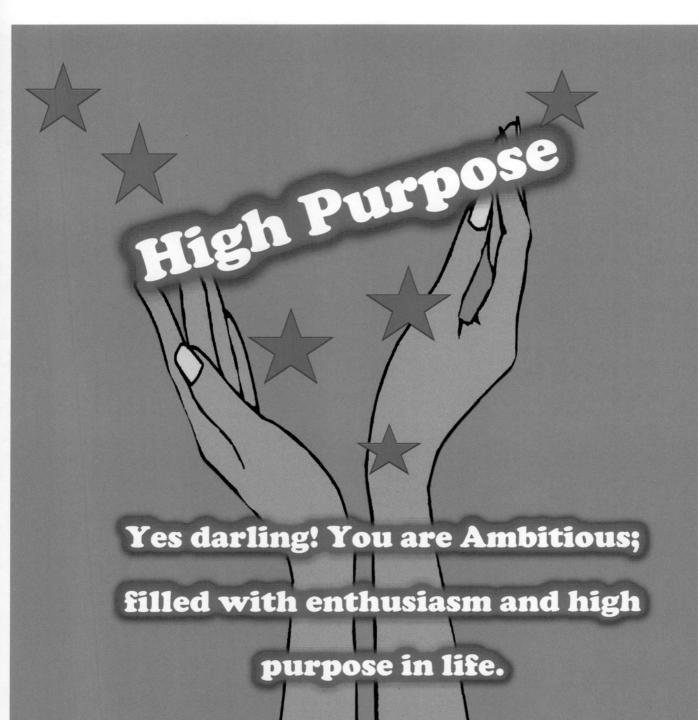

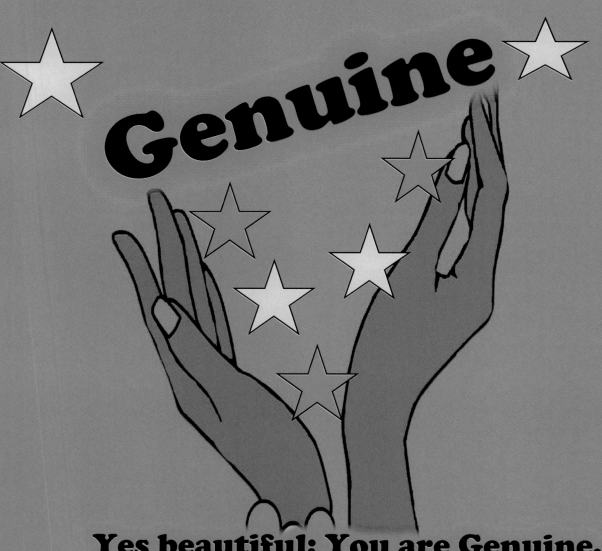

Yes beautiful; You are Genuine,

authentic and sincere.

Yes Chica; You are insightful; full of intuition and wise.

Amiable

Mommy, Do I have Black Girl Magic?

Yes Mija! You are Amiable; loving, supportive, and pleasant

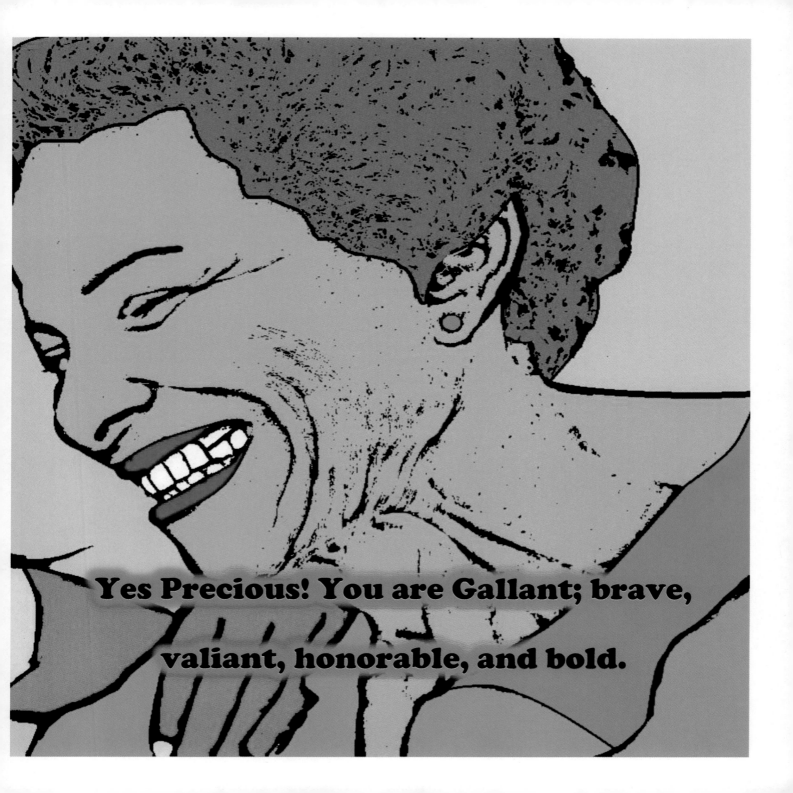

Yes Precious! You are Gallant; brave, valiant, honorable, and bold.

Made in the USA
Columbia, SC
28 September 2019